An Honorable Man

An Honorable Man

By Ruth Funk Jensen

iUniverse, Inc.
New York Bloomington

An Honorable Man

iUniverse books may be ordered through booksellers or by contacting:

iUniverse
1663 Liberty Drive
Bloomington, IN 47403
www.iuniverse.com
1-800-Authors (1-800-288-4677)

ISBN: 978-1-4401-9657-7 (sc)
ISBN: 978-1-4401-9658-4 (ebk)

Printed in the United States of America

iUniverse rev. date: 12/14/2009

In Memory of

Merle Funk

and dedicated to

Mike, Mary K. and Jean Anne

# Acknowledgements

My intention to write this tribute to my husband began more than thirty years ago. Kathe Bryant gave me the inspiration and encouragement to voice my thoughts. I express my thanks to her for helping me write, edit and bring life to my memories. I also appreciate the support of my children and friends in this venture.

Chapter 1

Looking back at the past, I recall many life altering moments. One day, April 29, 1977, was a day that would forever change my life. This particular day started out like any ordinary day, but would be burned in my consciousness forever.

My husband, Merle, who was a policeman, had just finished eating lunch. As he changed out of his uniform, he decided to go to a local men's club and play cards. As Chief of Police in a small town, he was on call twenty four hours a day and a few hours of relaxation would be good for him. Before going to the club, he decided to stop at the court house for a hearing about a local official who was to have charges placed against him. A local newspaper, known to manipulate and control politics in our county, had printed a headline story accusing an unnamed local official of theft and other misconduct. Of course, the story aroused everyone's interest. It was assumed the charges were against the incumbent judge by rivals who wanted to defeat him. While my husband was standing in the courtroom, waiting for the accused to be identified, he was horrified to learn the charges had been filed against him.

I was in the yard working on my rosebushes when I saw my best friend drive in. She had heard the news and came immediately to be with me. Waves of shock and disbelief swept over me. A few minutes later my husband arrived with an attorney friend. The look on my husband's face reminded me of an animal that had been shot and was suffering deep, deep pain. I will never forget the agonizing look on his face as long as I live.

The shock was emotionally and physically paralyzing for him. Friends started calling, all of them eager to offer support in any way they could. I felt so helpless and did not know how to ease Merle's pain. All I could do was to repeatedly tell him: "I love you." I do not know how we got through that dreadful April day. The following morning Merle resigned his job. That same day friends called and told him those were trumped up charges and no jury or judge in our state would convict him. Our friends came to visit; others called offering their support. Family members from out of state called and invited us to spend a few days with them. My husband chose to decline the invitations and led everyone to believe that he was fine. But I knew better. Never before had I seen him so terribly broken and discouraged.

Merle was curious to find out exactly how the charges against him were worded. He went to the courthouse and acquired a transcript. Much to his surprise, he found the charges against him had been filed and signed in September of 1976. He said: "Why would these charges be filed last year and court action taken seven months later?" He sighed and added: "Pud, this looks like a conspiracy."

Friday Merle told me he was going to our farm nine miles north of where we lived. As he had done many times in the past when he visited the farm, he took along his bird dog and gun to do some practice. When he left, he kissed me very tenderly, as he had in the past whenever he went on a business trip. My feelings were mixed when he left. I was afraid and worried and yet I knew he often worked out many of his problems when he was alone at the farm. When lunchtime arrived and he did not come home or call me, I became even more worried. The next four hours of waiting were torture. I can not describe the horror and fear I felt.

When the ambulance driver found Merle, he declared him dead. His death was ruled suicide. He had left a letter to the children and me telling us how much he loved us and asked our forgiveness. He told us the charges were not true and he believed it to be a conspiracy.

Within an hour after Merle's body was discovered at the farm, my house was full of people. Between friends, neighbors and relatives, there was not enough room to hold them in the house. They were on the porch and in the yard. One neighbor sent three bouquets of flowers in a twenty-four hour period. I was overwhelmed and did not know what to say or do. After my son and daughters arrived, I went to bed. Our family doctor came to sedate me so I could go to sleep. I was in a state of shock and do not recall who called him. The grief produced overwhelming pain, a pain worse than any labor pain. The shock to my system was devastating. I felt like I had been hit by a ten ton truck.

There was an investigation and the death certificate stated the cause of death as a self-inflicted gunshot wound. The days that followed were a blur for me.

Merle's best buddy from WW II, who lived in Chicago, came and helped make Funeral arrangements. He and Merle were such good friends that he offered to pay for Merle's funeral. Of course I refused, but was so touched by his offer.

There was a continuous line of family and friends during the six hour calling period at the funeral home. The outpouring of love from friends was overwhelming and there were over two hundred bouquets of flowers surrounding us. When Norman Weaver, our minister, started the service, his opening line was: "Another leader has fallen." Norman knew Merle personally from working together on an anti-drug program for the youth in the community.

I am a Christian and always thought I could forgive anything. However, forgiveness was not in my thoughts at that time. My thoughts toward the men whom I believed responsible for Merle's despair were very evil. I wanted to spit in their faces and do other wicked things to them. Had I been a person capable of such deeds, I would have been glad to serve time in prison. Instead, I leaned on my best friend, cried, yelled and acted plain crazy. I ended up in the hospital many times with what doctors called emotional burnout. During this terrible state of mind, I found it hard to talk to my children. They loved their father dearly and were hurting as much as I was.

How I longed to hear Merle's voice once more and hear him say: "My darling Pud." Pud was a nickname my four older brothers had given to me when I was very young. Merle picked up on it when we were dating. It continued to be his pet name for me. After Merle and I were married, no one else called me "Pud," not even my brothers. The very last time I was to experience that precious name was in the suicide note written by my husband.

I remember a few weeks after my husband's death there was a fire next door. It happened in the middle of the night and I heard the sirens and the firemen on my porch. The whole neighborhood was up and about. I was so depressed, I could not make myself get up. Even if my own house had been on fire, I would not have cared.

Words cannot express the mixed emotions of pain, frustration and rage, the children and I experienced over the following days, weeks, months and years. My son tried to deal with the pain and anger about his father's death by moving to California. One daughter gave up an opportunity for a promotion so she could be near me during this terrible time. Our other daughter, who already had chronic health problems, became even more ill.

I needed to go to work to support myself financially, which was a good thing. Thankfully, with the help of a good friend, I gained a suitable work position. Doctors Kathryn Mosier and Joseph Kerlin helped me survive during this unbearable time. And, by the grace of God and the help of relatives and friends, especially Joy Groover, I slowly began to put my life back together.

Politics should not be used to hurt others. People should run on their own merit. Why hurt others for our own gain? Are we not a Christian nation? Even now thirty one years later, the events surrounding my husband's death haunt me. It has taken me all this time to try to find forgiveness in my heart. There are days when I am not sure I have been completely successful in doing so. My prayer has been: "Lord, release me from this pain and please set me free." This book has been written as a catharsis for me, my family and dear friends.

Chapter 2

My parents were tobacco farmers in Kentucky. I was one of seven children and barely a year old when my family moved to Indiana in 1926. They bought a farm in Lizton, Indiana. My high school years were spent in Lizton and I was in my junior year when Japan attacked Pearl Harbor.

Merle Funk's life started in Casey, Illinois and he came from a large family too. One of eight children, he attended high school in the small town of Casey, Illinois. His favorite subject was debate and he dreamed of becoming a lawyer. However, in 1939 when he graduated, the Depression was still on and there was no money for college. So he moved to Indiana and found a job with General Motors.

In April of 1942, the Philippines surrendered to the United States. In June of that same year, with the help of the Navy, the United States defeated the Japanese in the Battle of Midway. * This was one of the turning points in the war.

In the fall of that same year, I was a senior in high school and almost 18. It was then I started dating Merle, who was four years older than I. At first the difference in our ages was a problem for my parents. They thought he was much too old for me. However, Merle was a charmer and soon Mother could not help but like him. In my eyes, he was absolute perfection. He was ever so handsome, reminding me of Jimmy Stewart, every time I looked at him. I could not help falling in love with his maturity and the gentle and loving way he treated me.

Merle and I were 'going steady' when he joined the Navy in October of 1942. This gentle, caring man was very interested in me. Before he left, he told me: "Ruth, I want you to enjoy your senior year and attend your last school year activities. Act your age even if it means dating someone else. However, while I am gone, I would like to think of you as 'my girl.' And, I hope you will consider yourself 'my girl' too." I loved it that he made no demands or conditions about our relationship, endearing him even more to me.

Impressed by his thoughtfulness, I had no desire to date anyone else. Merle was able to come home upon occasion because the Navy base was close to home and we both looked forward to those visits. When I graduated from Lizton High School in May 1943, Merle was stationed in Rhode Island. Although there was more distance between us now, he kept pursuing me. I was happy, because I had fallen deeply in love with him. In the summer of 1943, Merle purchased a set of wedding rings and I was filled with joy when this Navy sailor proposed marriage to me.

Our country was adjusting to the attack on Pearl Harbor and we were at war. Merle had a ten-day leave as he prepared to ship out. He kept asking me to make arrangements for a small wedding at my church, but I kept dragging my feet. His parents lived in a small town near Terre Haute. Merle invited me to go with him for a visit. Naturally, I was nervous about meeting them. I need not have worried, for I felt comfortable with his family from the very beginning. Merle's father had his own ideas as to our future and was not hesitant about voicing his opinion.

He said: "Merle and Ruth, in view of the situation our country is in, I think you should consider getting married now. You could go to Saint Louis and get married right away." My mind was racing and I felt numb. Married? Now? Of course, I did want to get married, but not so soon. Merle was in agreement with his father. In fact, I think he asked him to make that little speech. But, I had my reservations about rushing into marriage. Again, Merle's charm and persuasion erased my doubts.

After announcing the good news to my parents over the telephone, we were off to Saint Louis. On September 28, 1943, we stood in front of the Justice of the Peace and became husband and wife. I wore the one pretty dress I had with me. Suddenly, I was overcome with emotion and burst into tears.

"What is it? Why are you crying?"

"I don't have any flowers. No one is here. No family, no friends. No one saw us get married," I sobbed in a tearful voice.

In his usual compassionate fashion, Merle soothed my sorrow and fixed the one thing he was able to change. He lifted my spirits by bringing me a beautiful bouquet of flowers and taking me out to eat at a nice restaurant. Thus began our married life and I was now a war bride at age eighteen.

Like so many other young couples, the war separated us quickly. Only ten days after our marriage, he was on his way to California. Our honeymoon would have to wait. After my return home, I lived with my parents and worked at Allison Division, General Motors.

Three long months passed. Merle was stationed at Camp Parks, near San Francisco, California and wanted me to join him. I could not wait to be with my sweetheart, but did not have enough money to travel to California. My parents were unable to give me a loan. How was I going to pay for the trip? Then I told my brother, who was in the army, about my predicament. Thankfully, he was able to loan me enough money for the train passage.

I was so exited about being with my sweetheart and wanted to look just right for him. I needed shoes and after much begging, my sister gave me her ration stamps. I was wearing my wedding dress, a brown Chesterfield coat with velvet collar. Matching shoes and purse completed the outfit. My family took me to Union Station in Indianapolis.

It was a frightening, tearful time waiting on the train to come. I was bound for a place across the country. Having spent all my life on a farm near Lizton, Indiana, I knew nothing about travel or far away places. As I climbed the steps of the train, and looked back at my loved ones, a big knot formed in my stomach. I suddenly felt very alone, leaving the people who had made me feel secure all my life.

All the sleepers on the train had been taken, making my travels more difficult. I would be sitting up for the three days and nights it took to reach California. I was scared. As I looked out the window, a young lady holding a baby sat down next to me. She was already a mother at seventeen years of age. Looking at me dressed in my fancy new outfit, I probably appeared to be an experienced traveler. Little did she know how frightened and alone I felt. As the train moved closer to Chicago, we became better aquainted and shared stories of the war, our husbands and our hopes and fears about the future.

When we arrived in the Chicago train station, my new friend asked me to hold her baby while she found a place to heat the baby's bottle. She disappeared and I held the baby. As time wore on, I walked the baby for a while. Suzie had been gone for what seemed like a long time and a sense of unease was rising up inside of me. Here I was in Grand Central Station, holding a passenger's baby and wondering if she was ever coming back. I tried to have her paged, but since I did not know her last name, my request was denied. My mind was reeling with questions. What was I going to do? What if she did not come back? What would I tell my husband? How was I going to explain our being married just three months and here I was with a baby? Just as I was about to panic, Suzie reappeared with a warmed bottle of milk in hand. I was never so happy and relieved to see anyone!

Later I boarded the train in Chicago headed for the West Coast. The lovely outfit I wore to impress my husband was wrinkled and not fresh anymore. I had worn it around the clock and slept in it for three nights. As the train traveled west, I thought about my arrival in San Francisco. Just then, I heard women who were also meeting servicemen talking of departure at Oakland. Oakland! I did not remember Merle saying that. Now what was I going to do? My inexperience in travel left me with apprehension as I debated what to do.

Before I could think of what to do, the conductor was calling: "Oakland, Oakland next stop." I was fervently hoping that I was making the right choice when I stepped off the platform at Oakland. There was a crowd of women around me, all of them looking for their loved ones. I watched as couples reunited and my eyes anxiously searched the faces of the uniformed men. My heart skipped a beat when I suddenly saw my husband emerging from a crowd. We ran towards each other and embraced, just like in a movie scene. Finally we were together and all my fears vanished the moment we touched.

I was so filled with joy to be reunited with my husband, I have no memory of how we arrived at the room we rented in Livermore, California. The room was located in a rooming house run by nice, pleasant people. The following morning Merle was required to return to the Navy base. He had leave every three days. During his absence, I stayed in the room alone. Again, a rush of feelings washed over me. I was bewildered and lonely. What am I doing here? What am I going to do while Merle is away?

Soon, I discovered a public library and it became my sanctuary away from home. Books filled my days and allowed me to be in a world of my own during the long, lonely hours. One night I heard a noise in the room and a strange, unsettling feeling came over me, when I realized I was experiencing my first earthquake. The news of the event reached my family at home and with their usual concern, they worried for my safety. I told them: "Do not to worry about me. I am adjusting to my new life. As the wife of a United States Navy sailor, I am coping like thousands of other women in this country."

In the spring of 1944, Merle was transferred to Ventura, California and I followed. During October 23 to 26 of 1944, the United States naval forces destroyed the remains of the Japanese at the Battle of Leyte Gulf near the Philippines. This was the largest battle in history up to this point.*

---

* Midway Island, located in the North Pacific Ocean, near the northwestern end of the Hawaiian archipelago (2.4 square miles or 1,540 acres). Midway Island was a convenient refueling stop on transpacific flights and also an important stop for Navy ships.
Admiral Chester Nimitz took command of the devastated American Pacific Fleet at the end of 1941. He recommended the rebuilding of that force which became the most powerful fleet ever to sail the world's oceans. Nimitz shaped the strategy that led to Japan's ultimate defeat in 1945.
Midway's importance to the United States was brought into focus on December 7, 1941 with the Japanese attack on Pearl Harbor. Six months later, on June 4, 1942, a naval battle near Midway resulted in the U.S. Navy exacting a devastating defeat of the Japanese Navy. This battle of Midway was the beginning of the end of the Japanese Navy's control of the Pacific Ocean. Midway was also an important submarine base. ** The Battle of Leyte in the Pacific campaign of World War II was the invasion and conquest of Leyte in the Philippines by American (200,000 troops)

The time we spent together in California were months of bliss cut short when my husband was shipped to Hawaii. After tearful good-byes, I returned to Indiana to live with my parents. While waiting for the war to end, I worked at General Motors as a secretary.

Merle was trained as a construction worker ('Seabees') in the Navy and his unit would go in after battle to rebuild what had been destroyed. He was also the photographer for his battalion, so I often received pictures of beautiful U.S.O. entertainers such as Betty Hutton. With all those beautiful women around him, I sometimes wondered if I should be jealous, but Merle assured me there was no reason for that.

While stationed at Midway Island, the entertainer Joe E. Brown put on a show for the soldiers. U.S.O. entertainment was infrequent and life could get rather boring on Midway Island. The island was rich in wildlife. Seventy-three per cent of the world's Albatross (gooney birds) population resides on the island. One source of entertainment for the Seabees was to give whiskey to the gooney birds and watch them fall and get up.

Living in the Philippine Islands at Leyte was quite

---

and Filipino guerrilla forces (3,189) under the command of General Douglas McArthur, who fought against the Imperial Japanese Army (55,000 troops) in the Philippines led by General Tomoyuki Yamashita from October 17 to December 31, 1944. The battle launched the Philippines campaign of 1944-45 for the recapture and liberation of the entire Philippine Archipelago and to end almost three years of Japanese occupation.
Source: Wikipedia, the free encyclopedia

a culture shock for Merle. The natives, while quite charming, had little sense of decorum. Early on during his stay and unaccustomed to the native's ways, he often found himself surprised or embarrassed especially by the women. Once, while sitting on the Latrine, the door was suddenly opened from the outside. Looking down on him was a native woman, unclad from the waist up. With a big smile she asked: "Wanna buy bananas?"

When the war finally ended, a great weight was lifted from all of us. Once he was discharged from the navy, my husband returned to Lizton. I felt we finally could settle, begin our life as a married couple and raise a family.

When the war ended in August of 1945, we found a nice house in Lizton to rent. We lived there when our first child Michael Eugene Funk, was born January 20, 1947. We were ecstatic and he was the joy of our life. As he grew, he was full of energy and had questions about everything, People were drawn to him. Soon he played his first Little League game in Lizton. I will never forget how cute he looked in his uniform. His Dad and Howard Rogers organized the first Little League team in the town of Lizton. Before we knew it, Mike was in High School and played basketball and baseball. He excelled in sports.

Almost three years later, on November 16, 1949 our second child Mary K., who was named after both of our mothers, was born. She was a beautiful, shy baby with blond, curly hair. Mary soon outgrew her shyness and took tap dancing lessons. When she was five and six, she won several contests. She looked so adorable in her dance outfits. In 5th grade, she started playing the oboe and became quite accomplished. Winning several ribbons in State music competitions, she continued playing the oboe through high school. After attending a workshop for chosen music students from the Indianapolis area, she received special recognition at a concert at Butler University at age fourteen. Beautiful and intelligent, she brought many joys as well as challenges to our lives.

Two years and two months later, on January 25, 1952 our sweet Jean Ann was born. She was healthy and outgoing with enough energy for two children. In our neighborhood she was the leader of the youngsters and the organizer of games. She was multi talented, but was sent to the principal's office often while in grade school. No matter what happened, she always remained cheerful and optimistic. Jean was a tomboy, played softball, was active in 4-H and was on the student council in High School.

January 1944
Ruth and Merle in Ventura California

1944
Betty Hutton, entertaining troops at Midway Island

Joe E. Brown, entertainer at Midway Island

1944
Albatross (gooney) birds at Midway Island

1944
Betty Hutton at Midway Island

Mike, age 4

Mary K, age 9 months

Mary, age 3
Mike, age 6
Jean, age 1

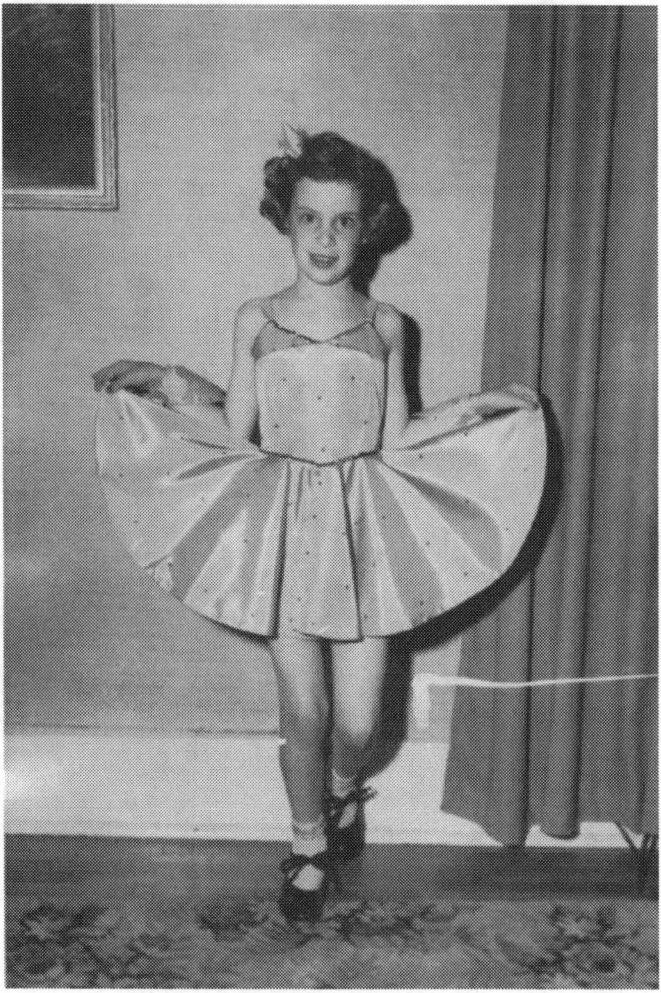

Mary K, age 5 ½

Chapter 3

By the 1950's, our family had grown to five. Our life in Lizton, Indiana was comfortable. Merle owned a filling station and garage. He was also part owner in the John Deere sales in town. Our children attended school in Lizton. All our needs were met and life was comfortable and happy.

Early in our marriage Merle gave me the responsibility of taking care of house hold bills. In those days, men usually handled the check book. I did not really want the responsibility of dealing with our finances, because I feared spending too much on the children and myself. Merle replied: "Well, if there is not enough to pay the light bill, we can always use candles." I wrote all the checks and he never had concerns or asked any questions about how I handled our finances. He trusted me and I was a good money manager.

Merle's business demanded much of his time and the kids and I were often alone. Soon Mike became old enough to spend time with his father at the station. Merle taught his son to value money early. He let him collect empty coke bottles earning Mike a little money. Merle would come home for lunch every day and he used part of this time to play or to talk to his children. They were happy and knew he loved them.

Reading to the children was one of my favorite

things to do. They loved it and so did I. Sometimes I felt lonely being tied down with the kids. Eventually my mother would stay with them on Saturday nights so Merle and I could spend time away from home or eat out at 'Frank and Mary's at Pittsboro. Our lives were simple in those days. We would take the children on a picnic or fishing. We would visit Merle's sister and friends in Illinois who lived on a big farm with a huge yard. During these visits the children had opportunity to go mushroom hunting, fishing, play croquet or play Grandma Funk's player piano.

We spent much time going to Mike's basketball and baseball games and attending Mary's music concerts. We watched Jean's soft ball games and enjoyed both girls' 4-H fairs projects.

When our daughter Jean was about ten years old, I would sometimes send her to the local grocery store to pick up an item or two. The store managers' names were Orville and Esther Johnston. Everyone in town knew and loved them. Orville had a magnificent personality and a wonderful smile. Jean had a crush on Mister Johnston and one day told his wife that she wanted to marry Orville!

Jean's dog was a border collie named Corky. He got much attention. Some evenings, when we entertained friends and relatives, Corky was the main attraction. Being in politics, Jean overheard much political discussion. Jean taught her dog the following trick. She would say: "Corky, which would you rather be: a democrat or a dead dog?" On the word 'dead,' Corky would lie down and play dead. This trick always resulted in much laughter.

My parents lived across the street from us in Lizton which made it convenient for all of us. My mother was so good to help me with the children. She raised seven children of her own and therefore had much experience. She rarely offered advice unless I asked for it. She was such a good woman and I miss her so much. Since my father had retired from farming, they had moved to town. They planted a garden and raised their own chickens. Having always worked so hard, they did not know how to slow down. My father began to lose his memory in the late 1950's. It was so very sad and my mother tried to take care of him by herself. When she finally confided how bad the situation was, Merle and I took turns spending the night with them so Mom could get some sleep. Dad would wander at night and try to leave the premises.

Soon, after consulting with the family doctor and the rest of the family, it was decided to place him in a facility where he would have consistent care. He was diagnosed with hardening of the arteries to the brain. It was one of the hardest days of our lives when we had placed him in a home. Being suddenly alone, Mother suffered. She suffered silently and seldom complained. She was of British ancestry and kept her feelings within. Perhaps she might have lived longer, had she been able to vent. She was raised by a stepmother who was partial to her own children. Mother said she never felt loved enough. Growing up, I often felt that way too, for she seemed preoccupied with her thoughts. I think she probably was thinking about how to make ends meet financially. We always had enough food, but she wanted to give us nice clothes as well.

One of the things I remember about Mother was her generosity. During the depression there were many hobos in our area. Since we lived only one mile from the railroad track in Lizton, hobos frequently knocked on our door. My mother always fed them, especially in the summer time when vegetables grew in abundance in our garden. We always had fresh milk, butter and cottage cheese. We churned our own butter and made cottage cheese. Usually Mother would have a piece of warm cornbread or a biscuit on hand to add to a hobo's meal.

We could never have imagined how a simple conversation with Republican County Chairman "Punch" Bradley, would change our lives. "Punch" asked Merle to run for Sheriff of Hendricks County. The offer sounded tempting. The two young men, who were working for Merle at the filling station, would be leaving for college soon. He was not looking forward to the task of training new men. Relocating to a larger school in Danville could provide more opportunities for the children. I was excited about this new adventure, yet torn about leaving my parents who lived close by. We did move to Danville, but kept the door of returning open, by renting rather than selling our home in Lizton. A new chapter was opening for the entire Funk family.

The political life we were about to enter was completely new to us. Merle filed for the office of Sheriff in 1958 running against the incumbent Leon Bayliss. Merle was the underdog in the race. He was not well known and had little experience when it came to politics. Therefore, it was not surprising that he lost his first attempt in being elected Sheriff of Hendricks County.

When Sheriff Bayliss could not run again for office due to term limits, Merle filed again for another try at the office. He became one of five candidates. This time he was better known and had made many local friends. Our family campaigned throughout the county. This time, in January of 1963, Merle Funk became Sheriff of Hendricks County. Merle was to serve two four year terms. At the time of his election, he was 42 and I was 38. Our children's ages were Mike 15, Mary K.13 and Jean Ann 10.

On New Year's Eve, December 31, 1963, we began our life in Hendricks County Jail. The experience ahead was uncharted waters for us. The large, beautiful brick building was built in 1876. The county was very small back then, housing the occasional prisoner. During that era, the Sheriff was the ultimate authority in law enforcement in each county. Therefore, the living quarters provided, were very elegant.

The jail where the prisoners stayed was attached to our living quarters. The walls between rooms were made of brick and about four inches thick. The original window shutters, hanging from ceiling to floor, provided either light or privacy. As we entered through the large doors, the spiral staircase greeting us in the entryway reminded me of the one in the movie 'Gone with the Wind.' To the left of the main doors was a small area designated as the sheriff's office. It was wall papered, had a telephone, radio for dispatch, a desk, chair and another chair for visitors. The sheriff used the office in the evenings and on weekends. During the weekdays, the sheriff was at his office in the courthouse.

Before it was converted to steam heat, the building was heated by wood. Now, the living room was the only remaining fireplace in the home. The main floor also housed a huge kitchen with walk-in pantry and a dining room. Merle and I occupied the only bedroom and bath on this floor. It had been added many years after the original construction of the house. At the end of the hall, next to the kitchen, was a door leading to the jail area. Upstairs were three bedrooms that the children occupied. A family bathroom was also upstairs. The bathroom had no ceiling and opened to the roofline. Few structural changes were made during the eight years our family lived there.

The heating system was steam with old-fashioned registers that clinked and clanged every time the heat kicked on. The first night of our stay there, we were awakened at midnight by the sound of clanging metal. We were certain a jailbreak must be in progress!

Our new lifestyle was quite an adjustment. However, after a few weeks of living in the 'county jail,' life began to feel normal again. The children were within easy walking distance of their respective schools. They made many friends and hosted parties at the Sheriff residence. Jean Ann entertained girl friends with a slumber party and as the girls left, they were fingerprinted and turned over to the custody of their parents. Mike could be heard playing Ping-Pong late into the night as Merle and I tried to sleep in the room above the table. Mary K. and Jean Ann walked down the spiral staircase in their prom dresses and all three of the children graduated from high school while in the grand home.

Our daughter Mary played the oboe through junior high and high school. When she entered the state contests, she won many blue ribbons. In her freshman year at the Christmas program, I remember she and the drummer had a solo part playing 'The Little Drummer Boy.' The auditorium was packed. The piece was so moving, you could hear a pin drop.

Sometimes our home was filled with teenagers, policemen, an assistant cook, the press, a food salesman, a state jail inspector, our dog Corky and whoever else might be there for one reason or another. It was hectic, but one of the best times in our lives.

In the beginning Merle had two deputies. By virtue of my being married to the Sheriff, I became the official jail matron. I was deputized and issued a uniform and badge. However, I refused to carry the gun that would have completed my attire.

My duties included the oversight of the women prisoners. It was my responsibility to search them, accompany them to court appearances, transfers to women's prison, hospitals or mental health facilities. The Sheriff or one of the gun carrying deputies would accompany me on these trips.

One day a woman arrested for intoxication was brought to the jail. As was required of me, I took her watch, rings and other personal items. After placing them in an envelope, I locked them in the safe. The following day we brought her before a judge who declared the amount of her fine. He said: "Since you do not have money for bail, I have no choice but to send you back to jail." The woman laughed and replied: "I have plenty of money." She promptly reached down her brassier and pulled out a roll of bills. She muttered: "Your stupid matron didn't frisk me very well, did she?"

After this experience, I made sure I would not make the same mistake again. The next woman I frisked. I looked down her blouse and asked: "What have you got down there?" Her reply was: "The same thing you have, honey."

When we first took office, a lovely lady by the name of Mayme Gentry had been the cook. She was only able to work two days a week. She loved to cook and would bake pies for the prisoners even though our budget did not allow much for extras like pies. The prisoners loved her pies and would want to stay forever. Our children had tasted her pies and each had their favorite. Soon she was baking their favorite pies. They would thank her and give her a big hug. She spoiled the kids and was like a second grandmother to them.

I also washed the blankets and towels of the inmates. Another one of my many jobs was to plan the prisoners' meals, buy the groceries, and cook for the prisoners three times a day, seven days a week. The county provided two freezers, which were located in the basement. I kept a financial record of the food purchased. The cost was to be fifty cents for each meal. It took quite a bit of calculating, because if I ran over the allotted cost figure, it came out of our personal finances.

Breakfast was usually coffee, doughnuts and fruit. Lunch, the main meal of the day, might be chili, beans and corn bread, or spaghetti, a vegetable and fruit. In the evening, the meal was lighter such as a sandwich, soup and cookie. Generally, I prepared a separate meal for our family. My husband was diabetic, requiring a special diet, my three hungry teenagers were fussy eaters, and I was pre-menopausal! High stress levels became a way of life. My load was lightened somewhat, when Merle asked the county to provide a portable dishwasher for the residence.

The jail was old and very depressing. The prisoners had separate steel frame beds with foam rubber mattresses, a blanket and a pillow. They did like my cooking. The meals were adequate, nutritious, and cooked fresh daily.

There came a time when I appealed to the County commissioners for assistance and was told there were no extra funds. Eventually, help was hired, but it was paid from my $360 per month pay. Once Imogene Ayers was hired she helped me with the prisoners' meals during the week. Imogene was a lovely lady and worked with me during the eight years we stayed at the Sheriff residence. She was efficient, neat and a very good cook. I really appreciated her help.

The deputies who worked with Merle during those eight years included Bill Berzyne, "Red" Downerd who did office work, John Carico, Marvin Wills, Jim Morris, Ray Hubbard, Lee Taylor and others. There was often talk pertaining to the tunnel, which runs from the courthouse to the boiler room for transporting prisoners. I know of no time that this happened during my husband's term as Sheriff.

Occasionally we took family vacations. Whenever we left someone had to come in and stay the night with the prisoners. Once we spent a week at a cottage at Racoon Lake, but an emergency arose and Merle was called back to work.

Having three children in school, my husband and I attended our son's basketball and baseball games, our daughter's band concerts, Four-H events and other school activities.

Since my husband's job was political, I had to attend political meetings, fundraisers, Women's Republican Club, etc. All of these activities made it difficult to have quality time with family. We tried to have as normal a life as possible and connected every day by eating dinner together. We encouraged the children to have parties, sleepovers and other teen-age activities. They were popular with their peers and their friends were always welcome in our home.

Later, when Mike was in college, he would call and ask if he could bring home some fraternity brothers for dinner. It was usually short notice, but I always said 'yes' and we had a fun time together.

Merle's term as Sheriff ended December 31, 1971. The day we left the jail, it was with mixed emotions. Our children had all graduated from High School and were in college. One was working for the Federal Bureau of Investigations. We had moved back to our home on W. Mill Street. What a drastic change! We had been used to prisoners to feed, telephone calls during the night, disruption around the clock and a house full of kids. The house was now so empty and quiet.

Merle took a few days off from work trying to decide where his career would go from there. After much discussion and assessing our financial needs, he accepted a job as Chief of Police in Danville.

Our son Mike graduated from Indiana State University in Terre Haute with a degree in Business Marketing. He worked in sales for many years. His first job was as purser on a cruise ship in the Caribbean.

Mary K. graduated from Southern Oregon College with a degree in Education. She spent her first two years in Japan where she taught English to people age six to sixty in a private school. After her return to the states, she continued teaching in a private school in Midtown Manhattan.

Jean chose not to go to college. She was in Federal Bureau of Investigations training and had hopes of being the first female agent. But, a lack of patience and homesickness cut her studies short and she returned to Indiana. She is a professional photographer with her own business in Columbus Indiana and one of the happiest people I know.

With the children grown up and gone, and our mortgage paid off, I decided to work part time in the courthouse. I worked in a local bank and later, part time in the Indiana Legislature.

Our first house purchased in 1953

May 1962
Merle Funk family on election night

May 1962
Election Night

Mary K, age 17

Mike, age 18

STATE OF INDIANA
OFFICE OF THE GOVERNOR
INDIANAPOLIS

ROGER D. BRANIGIN
GOVERNOR

June 27, 1967

Merle Funk
Sheriff of Hendricks County
Hendricks County Jail
Danville, Indiana

Dear Sheriff Funk:

Thank you for accepting an appointment as a member of the Law Enforcement Training Board. I am certain you share my concern that this important area receive a careful and thorough analysis by men, such as yourself, dedicated to the highest possible degree of excellence in police services.

The initial meeting of the Board will be held on Tuesday, July 11, 1967, at 2:00 p.m. in the State Police Conference Room (305 State Office Building) in Indianapolis. A more detailed agenda and information on your commissioning will be forwarded in the very near future.

With best wishes, I remain

Sincerely,

Roger D. Branigin
Governor of Indiana

RDB:ed

Merle and his deputies

HEADQUARTERS
INDIANA STATE POLICE
INDIANAPOLIS

OFFICE OF THE SUPERINTENDENT

July 3, 1967

Mr. Merle Funk
Sheriff of Hendricks County
Danville, Indiana 46122

Dear Merle:

Congratulations on your appointment to the Law Enforcement Training Board by Governor Branigin.

As ex-officio chairman of the Board, I have called the first meeting at 2 p.m., Tuesday, July 11, 1967. It would be greatly appreciated if you could arrange to attend this meeting since we would like to take a photograph of the entire Board. Likewise, I wish to appoint committees to go to work on this program as soon as possible.

In my opinion, this is the finest thing that has ever happened to law enforcement in Indiana. I know by working together much can be accomplished for law enforcement in Indiana.

Sincerely,

Robert A. O'Neal
Superintendent

RAO:dp

Editorials

Thinking Big

Hendricks county should be proud of the fact that it is going to be the home of the new Indiana Police Training Academy.

A lot of people worked very hard to get this accomplished, too many to single out by name. However, we cannot overlook the fact that Hendricks County Sheriff Merle Funk was an active member of the Site Selection Committee and never gave up hope despite earlier selection of another site.

Perhaps one of the major keys to the success of this project was the fact that many people in this county thought big. Instead of thinking in terms of communities, they thought in terms of county.

Too long, our county has been stagnated by selfish ideas of community first, county second. Too many failed to look beyond their own city limits, refusing to believe that something which would benefit the county, would benefit all communities.

True, Plainfield will be the mailing address of the new academy, but Plainfield is still a part of Hendricks county. If more people will adopt the bigger attitude, our county can expect to become more attractive to industry and other desirable developments.

senger--Monday, July 28, 1969

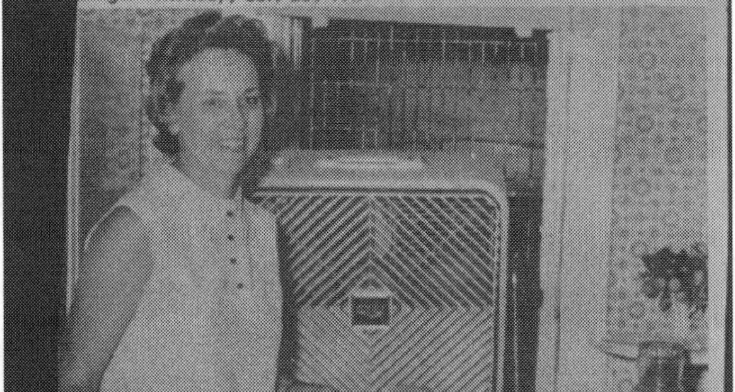

Mrs. Merle Funk, prepares the noon meal for inmates at the county jail.

FRONT COVER PHOTO

In a grand move all the police associations have gotten together to back a proposal for a police training academy and to enact a mandatory police training bill. The State Police Photo on the cover shows the police officials who met in Indianapolis recently to discuss the plans which are going before the 1967 legislature. James Naugle is with SAC (Federal Bureau of Investigation); Merle Funk with the Hendricks Co. Sheriff's Department (Sheriff's Association); and Stephen Ranich of the Highland Chief of Police (Chief's Association). Those in the top row are: Fred Swago, Captain of the Indianapolis Police Department (F.O.P.); Kenneth Chaney, New Whiteland Chief of Police (Police League); and Robert O'Neal, Supt. of the Indiana State Police. For a story on the proposal before legislature see page 7.

INDIANA JUSTICE: An Indianapolis gent with a long record was trying to burglarize a store in Danville. The owner shot him full of buckshot, but his partner-in-crime got away. Burglar was taken to Hendricks County Hospital and placed under $5000 bond. He quickly managed to dig up $500 to pay bondsmen so he could get out. However, Sheriff **M e r l e Funk** wouldn't accept it until the hoodlum paid a $131 hospital bill.

Chapter 4

My husband Merle was a kind, considerate man, a gentle soul, who cared deeply about his family and everyone who touched his life. He treated the prisoners with dignity and respect. During his counseling, he would tell them: "Someone thinks you have broken the law or you would not be here. This is not a good place to be, but if you obey the rules, I will treat you well. Some of your privileges have already been taken away from you. If you ignore the rules, you will lose more privileges. For example, I may have to refuse to let you have visitors or cigarettes. You can create a life that is tolerable, or one that is miserable. It is up to you and the choices you make."

Merle received a report about a break-in at New Winchester High School that had closed because of consolidation with Danville. When he arrived there, he found a group of young men playing basketball inside. It was a rainy, damp day and the boys had jimmied the lock so they could stay dry playing basketball. Merle took out his note pad and wrote down the names and ages of the boys. When the matter became public, a father and his son appeared at the Sheriff's office to see if his son's name was on the list. Instead of showing the man the list, he told him that on his way home he had the car window down, and the list flew out the window. Kind-hearted as he was, Merle did not want the boys to have to appear in juvenile court for a minor misconduct that could be settled out of court.

Over the years, very few prisoners refused to cooperate. When Merle saw a need, he always attempted to fix it and most of the time his efforts were successful. There was a large supply cabinet for the prisoners containing personal items such as toothpaste. There was also a shelf for stamps, stationary, candy and donated magazines. The prisoner's family or friends provided personal laundry and other personal supplies.

During the years Merle was sheriff, the local hospital did not have facilities for the mentally ill and often they would be brought to Henricks County Jail to be locked up. Such prisoners should have been restrained to protect themselves as well as those around them. Putting the mentally ill in jail only added to their confusion and frustration. This problem weighed heavily on Merle's mind. Working together with a civic-minded businessman named Bob Jensen and the County Mental Health Association, the hospital agreed to install security lock ups with padded cells for the mentally ill. Merle worked with hospital administrators to provide as much security as his staff would allow.

Often, when prisoners were released, I would watch Merle reach into his own pocket to give them bus fare to Indianapolis. Families in dire need never left the Sheriff's office empty handed.

Through the years not too many women prisoners stayed at the jail. Most were incarcerated for small things such as shoplifting or public intoxication. One girl I remember was a 19-year-old Indiana University student from Brownsburg who was accused of 2nd degree manslaughter in the death of her newborn child. While awaiting her trial, she spent seven months in jail. Her attorney was John Vandiver and eventually she was acquitted.

While most events having to do with inmates were rather serious, some of our experiences had a humorous side. Before the communication system was moved to the jail, we took all calls all night long. One night after we had gone to bed, Merle took a call from a woman complaining about an abusive husband. She did not want to file charges, she just wanted to complain. Merle recognized her from previous calls. Since the situation required no action, I tried to go back to sleep. After a while I realized Merle had stopped talking and all of a sudden, I heard him snoring. When I glanced over at him, he was still holding the telephone to his ear. We never heard from the woman again, at least not at 3:00 A.M.

Oh, the life of a small county Sheriff. It was hectic, funny, sad, educational and at times very rewarding. We had many unusual experiences. I am so sorry Merle's life had to end the way it did. He had so much to offer. I still miss him after all these years. After being alone for twenty years, I remarried. Bob Jensen was a very nice man from Danville and we had eight wonderful years together before he passed away.

Many prisoners came and went. Some have stayed in my mind more than others. One Cartersburg man, Keith Wright, we came particularly fond of. He was in jail for a few months and during a conversation with him, Merle heard about Keith's interest in art. Keith, an introverted person, loved to paint in oils. While serving his time, Merle made it possible for him to paint a large mural, which we donated to the museum. Today the mural is on display in the male cell area. Keith also painted individual portraits of our children and one of Merle and I. We were proud of the wonderful painted likenesses, and I still display them in my home. Merle had a talent for bringing out the best in the prisoners and had a positive impact on them.

Merle Funk was the first sheriff to hire a woman. Susan Austin, became clerk and later a deputy. She became a strong leader in assisting abused women.

One day a high school student walked in our front door without knocking. She was very hostile and insisted on talking to the Sheriff immediately. We discovered later she was having severe mental problems. Merle and I were to transport her to Logansport State Mental Institution. I was afraid, but Merle knew how to keep her calm. He told her when she got out of the institution, he would help her find a job so she could be independent. This pleased her. She calmed down and by the time we reached our destination, she even began to like both of us. I am not sure how or if she was released.

Another memory that stands out is the trip to Texas to pick up a run-away fifteen year old girl. Her reason for leaving home was that her stepfather was sexually abusing her while her mother worked nights. When she finally worked up the courage to tell her mother, she refused to believe her. Desperate, the young girl took in ironing and baby-sat until she had saved enough money to travel to Texas by bus. After her arrival, she located her boyfriend who was in the military service. He did not know she was coming, nor was he aware of her problem. Since she was a minor, he took her to the authorities and we were called.

Merle and I were ordered by the court to bring her home. The first stop on our way back was in Northern Texas where we had to put her in jail over night. The next morning she told us her jail cell had been full of cockroaches. We were planning to drive all the way home the next day. However, when we reached Illinois, we encountered a snow storm. We kept her in a motel room joining ours. After all, she was not a criminal, but a victim of a crime. She was a nice girl. Upon her return, the court took her away from her abusive home and placed her in the care of a relative. I wished we could have kept her with us, but of course that was not possible. I cannot remember, but I believe her step-father was found guilty and convicted. If she should read this, I hope her life turned out well and happy in spite of her unfortunate experiences.

Sheriff Funk and a few volunteers accomplished the forming of the first organization of 'Reserve Deputies' for Hendricks County. These men assisted with paperwork, becoming a turnkey and riding with the deputies for extra protection. The men organized fund-raisers such as wrestling matches and country and western singers. They raised enough money to buy their own uniforms and never accepted any money for their efforts.

Prior to being Sheriff, much of Merle's time was spent with Little League Baseball. He truly loved those boys. Many of them have told me what an impact he had made on their lives. He was a man who believed in the youth of our community and made efforts to maintain their safety. Together, with the Danville Ministerial Association, Merle formed a drug awareness program to keep young people off drugs.

Merle and Bob O'Neal, former sheriff of Marion County and Indiana State Police Superintendent, were instrumental in getting the Indiana Law Enforcement Academy built in Plainfield. I remember the long hours and how he spent his own money on this project. The idea began with Merle and Bob. Our families were good friends. One evening when they were visiting us the men were discussing the low pay for police and how little was required of them to become eligible for a deputy sheriff position. They took the discussion to the Indiana Sheriffs Association. Through their efforts a bill was eventually introduced into Indiana Legislature and passed in both houses. The Governor signed the bill and it became a law. It was now mandatory for all policemen, deputies, town marshals and conservation officers to have a certain number of weeks of training and to pass a test before they could be licensed as officers. Merle was a charter member of the Board of Directors. With deep conviction in this endeavor, he and a twelve-member board spent many months of preliminary work establishing this project, all without any financial benefit.

Merle worked diligently to help people in need. I recall an incidence when a man who had lost his job came to see him. He told him how he had lost his job and needed fuel to heat his home. The man was too proud to go to the Welfare Department. He wanted to make it on his own and find another job. Merle gave the man money out of his pocket to pay the fuel bill.

Living at the prison was a good experience for our children. It showed them first-hand what it was like to be incarcerated. They learned not only about confinement, but also about the loss of personal freedom, privileges and conveniences. It showed them how much in their lives they took for granted. Even though he may not have expressed his ideals in words, he taught our children by example. Watching his caring and helpful attitude towards the prisoners showed them how to be respectful and helpful towards other people. By their father's example they learned to respect human beings regardless of their situation or what they may have done in the past. I am so grateful he was with them long enough to teach them these important life lessons.

I am now 84 years in age (I refuse to say old). And, I am grateful for my longevity and all my <u>good</u> life experiences. Dr. Wayne Dyer is one of my favorite authors and he states: 'What goes around comes around.' According to Dr. Dyer, people who commit evil must live with that evil. If I were to choose to remain bitter about what happened, I would only hurt myself. So, I am not bitter anymore.

Our son Mike had a tree planted in his father's honor at the Danville Park. The fully grown white sycamore tree is a constant reminder of all the time Merle spent with the youth of Danville. Sitting in the park, looking at the trees on beautiful fall days, I remember the past. All the good times the youth and our entire family had here at the park come to life in my mind.

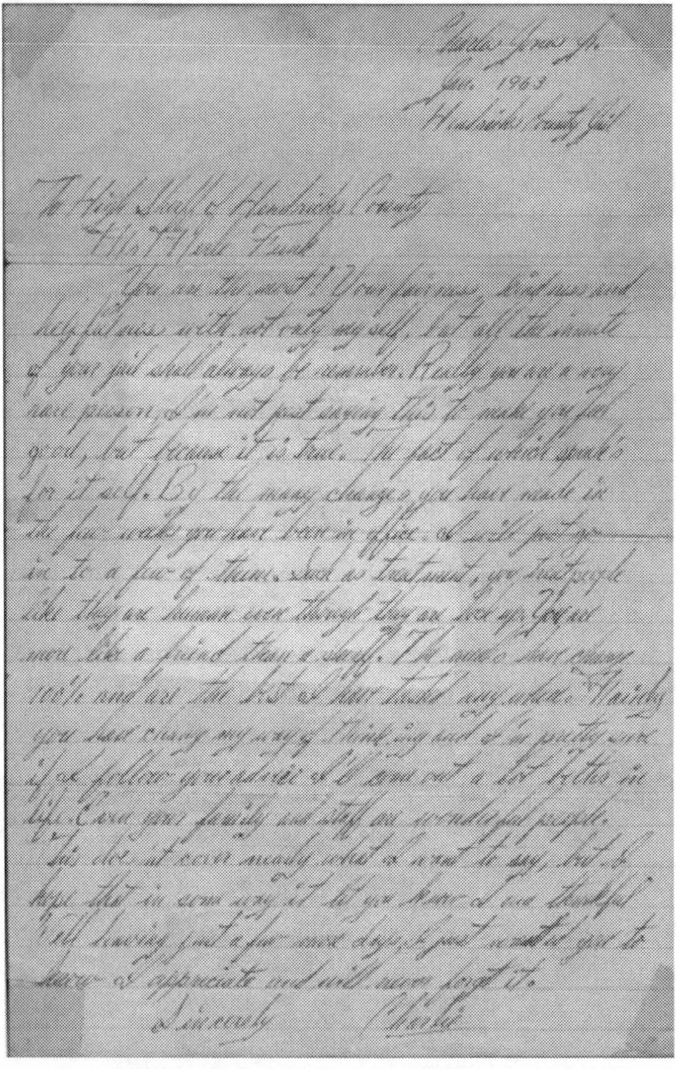

Charles Jones Jr.
Jan. 1963
Hendricks County Jail

To High Sheriff of Hendricks County
Mr. Wade Frank

You are the most! Your fairness, kindness and helpfulness with not only myself, but all the inmate of your jail shall always be remember. Really you are a very nice person, I'm not just saying this to make you feel good, but because it is true. The fact of which speak's for it self. By the many change's you have made in the few weeks you have been in office. I will point up in to a few of them. Such as treatment, you treat people like they are human even though they are lock up. You are more like a friend than a sheriff. The meal's have always 100% and are the best I have tasted any where. Really you have chang my way of thinking and I'm pretty sure if I follow your advice I'll come out a lot better in life. Even your family and staff are wonderful people.

This letter doesn't nearly what I want to say, but I hope that in some way it let you know I am thankful. I'll leaving just a few more days, I just wanted you to know I appreciate and will never forget it.

Sincerely Charles

Letter of appreciation from Hendricks County Jail

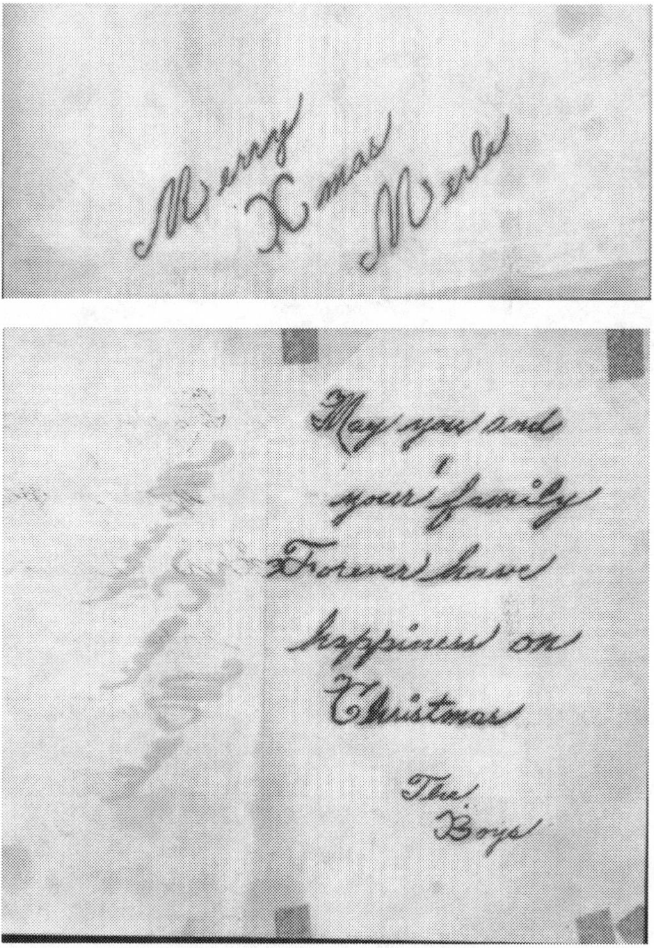

Christmas Card from Inmates

Jean Anne and Corky

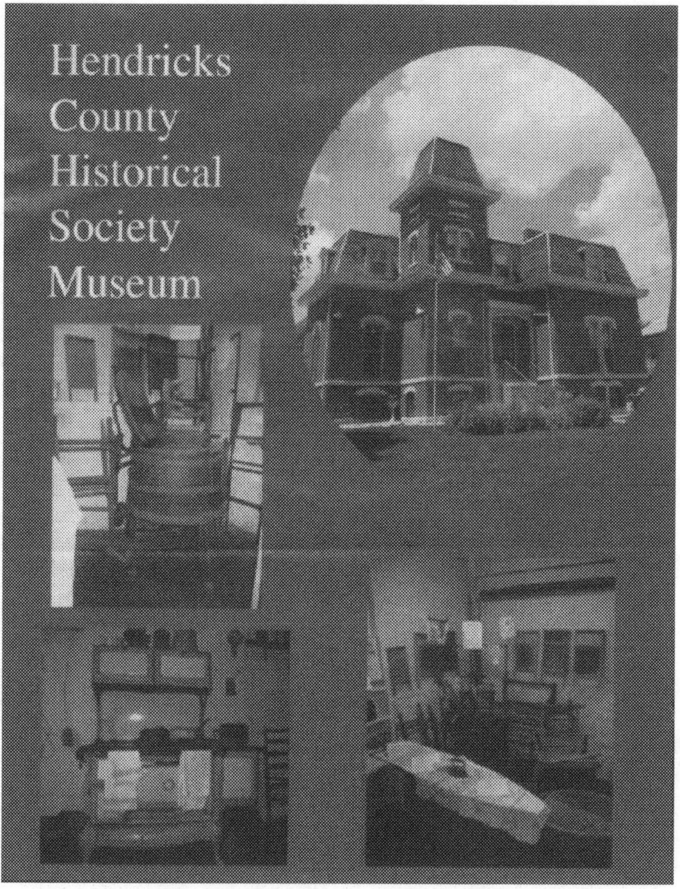

Former Hendricks County Jail

Epilogue

"The history of the world is the history of control by institutions, individuals and ideas."

Marianne Williamson: Illuminata, page 12

In reviewing the pages of my past, I cannot help but contemplate how different our family's lives would have been had my husband lived. I can hardly imagine the depth of pain and humiliation Merle must have suffered to end his life. He was a humble and fair man and never sought recognition for all the good he did for others. When he saw a need, it was second nature to him to step up and attempt to fix it.

The Sycamore tree in the park stands as a reminder of Merle's love for the youth of the community. It saddens me to think of how much more good Merle could have done during the years to come. Thinking of the joys he missed as his children grew saddens me even more.

The pain of his loss will always be with the children and me. My dreams of growing old together were buried with him.

My husband was a fair man. Unfortunately, when it comes to politics there is no fairness. Once politicians gain power and control, they often lose sight of their humanity and moral obligations. There are different standards of happiness, ethical: enduring happiness throughout a lifetime, and psychological: momentary satisfaction of wants and desires. Sometimes short-term benefits are seized at the cost of long-term evils.

My purpose of writing this biography is to make the reader aware of how personal greed can deeply hurt and even destroy another person and their family. I hope people will learn from this tragedy and become kinder and more considerate of one another.